LEFT SHOE

and the Foundling

Annie O'Dowd

NATIONAL
MARITIME
MUSEUM

When you see this flower
in the story, turn to Marigold's
Dictionary on page 73.

1
About Seadogs

LET ME TELL YOU about the seadogs. You probably haven't heard of us, because humans hardly ever see a seadog. We live by the sea in complex burrows near the sand. We are cheerful and social by nature, but also shy, especially of humans. Perhaps you have noticed a little driftwood door under a tree, or seen a scurry of brown fur out of the corner of your eye. Once I saw some humans pick up a pair of seadog trousers forgotten on the sand and marvel at their small hand-stitched seams. They must have puzzled over the round hole at the back, which is, of course, for the seadog's stumpy tail. Humans, as far as I know, don't have tails.

Seadog burrows are hidden. They are nestled into the grasses, secreted under rocks and obscured by shady trees. These underground homes are always by the sea. They are gathered in villages, which are dotted here and there along coastlines around the world. I would draw you a map, but I'm not really sure of their exact locations. I only know that we are often visited by seadogs from other villages, sometimes from lands across the sea.

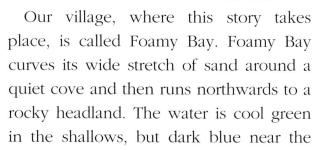

Our village, where this story takes place, is called Foamy Bay. Foamy Bay curves its wide stretch of sand around a quiet cove and then runs northwards to a rocky headland. The water is cool green in the shallows, but dark blue near the horizon, where the wind blows the tops of the waves into foamy peaks. On the edge of the beach, many little boats are pulled up next to the protection of spreading casuarina trees. Under their pale branches is a tangle of burrows. These smooth mounds are built on both sides of a narrow river. Altogether there are twenty-three families in Foamy Bay village, a total of two hundred and thirty-eight seadogs at last count.

Although the entrances to our homes are well concealed, inside they are rather like human houses. There is a kitchen, sitting room and fireplace. Seadogs cook their food on a wood-burning stove. We use pots and plates just as you do!

In a burrow like this live Blue Bottle and Old Cork Sandburrow. You might think these names sound strange, but you will soon learn the special way in which we seadogs receive our names.

Blue Bottle and Old Cork's cosy burrow lies behind a low, sloping sand dune beneath some casuarina trees. Their small driftwood front door is only about the size of your school desk. When opened, a round room is revealed. Small circular windows lighten it by day. At night, candles or lanterns spread their warm glow. There is a scrubbed kitchen table and a colourful rug on the floor. The earth walls are painted with whitewash and decorated with all kinds of things found at the edge of the sea: bits of old rope, fishing net and useful pieces of plastic are carefully placed between family portraits. There are cabinets stuffed with books. Against one wall sits a jumbled row of sacks. These contain grass-seed flour or seaweed sugar.

Baskets of dried fish and sea vegetables are stacked under a sturdy wooden bench by the window, where a shutter is usually pushed open to the breeze. There are comfy chairs arranged around the warm iron stove. On the opposite side of the little room, which seadogs call a snug, a tunnel leads to darker parts of the burrow. It is altogether a delightful home, comfortable and safe. I wish you could see such a place, but it's rare for a human child ever to meet a seadog.

It is here in this burrow that the story begins. It is a very exciting story in which you will meet the most carnivorous creature in the ocean: a monster so gruesome and dangerous that you will be frightened out of your wits – the giant squid! The giant squid lives in the deepest, coldest parts of the ocean and can grow up to twenty metres long. Its great eyes are the largest of any creature in the world. This mysterious animal has eight arms lined with round suckers, which can stick to your body like suction cups. Concealed in the suckers are rows of claw-like barbs, which help the squid to clasp its prey. I know all this because I've seen one, so believe me when I tell you that the giant squid has an extra two arms called tentacles. These tentacles are twice as long as the whole creature and can snatch their victim with terrifying speed. On the end of each tentacle is a club, and on each club are four rows of suckers armed with barbed hooks. The dreadful giant squid can also coil the long, feeding tentacles together and use the clubs as

snapping jaws! Once it has the struggling creature in its grasp, the vile squid eats it.

Can you imagine anything more abominable? Its dark and slimy mouth lies underneath its legs. I would like to describe the sharp beak, the only tooth of this horrendous mollusc, but I don't want to give you bad dreams.

The giant squid has one fear – whales. Some whales have been known to attack and eat giant squid. The two mighty creatures have been seen at sea, fighting to the death. The giant squid sometimes wins the battle. The dreadful monster wraps its tentacles around the whale, holding the poor mammal under the water

6

until it drowns. The giant squid has other prey, too. Using its gigantic eyes to hunt in the blackness of the ocean floor, it gorges itself on glowing deep-sea fish. But the giant squid's favourite food of all is the small, brown seadog. Seadogs dread this creature above all others, as it can cast its ten-metre-long tentacles onto the sand and snatch a tender pup for tea.

I'll tell you one more thing, but I hope you will be able to sleep tonight. The giant squid glows.

This story reveals the bravery of one particular seadog. His name is Left Shoe. The story starts sadly, I'm sorry to say, and it begins on the day Left Shoe was born.

2
Left Shoe is Born

ON THAT ILL-FATED morning, Blue Bottle was put to bed to have her babies. She knew it would be twins, one boy and one girl, because that's the way it always happens with seadogs. Blue Bottle's husband, Old Cork, was making sure everything was ready. Through the small open window they could see a grey film of rain sweeping across the sea. Old Cork pulled the window shut and turned to Blue Bottle. She smiled at him as he squeezed her paw in encouragement.

When evening came at the end of that long, damp day, Blue Bottle gave birth to her twins. The first, a healthy boy, barked loudly and waved his paws. The next, a pale brown girl, made no sound, and died quietly. She never opened her eyes. Old Cork tucked her into a separate basket and lit a candle for her. Sorrow filled the silence that followed. Then, Old Cork comforted his wife as she wept.

The next morning, Blue Bottle and Old Cork carried their pups to the beach to name them. New babies are always named at sunrise. They are named after the most special piece of treasure discovered on the tide line that morning. When I say treasure, I don't mean gold coins or jewels found in an old chest, I mean seadog treasure! This includes any interesting objects washed onto the beach by the sea.

But as Blue Bottle and Old Cork surveyed the wet sand, there was only one thing drifting on the water's edge, pushed in and then sucked out a little by the tide. It was a left shoe. An ordinary shoe like your father might wear, only cracked and hardened

9

by the salt. It had long since lost its shoelace and had become the home of a rather bad-tempered hermit crab. When the shoe was retrieved, the crab scuttled away, angrily shaking its claw.

'I name you Left Shoe,' said Old Cork, gazing down at his new son. 'Welcome, Left Shoe, to the Sandburrow family.'

Blue Bottle's tears began to fall again, as there was no treasure for the other little baby.

'There must be something on the shore for her,' she said sadly. The small, still girl lay in her arms. Old Cork saw a broken shell at Blue Bottle's feet. It was striped with many colours.

'I name you Broken Shell,' he said.

The next day, Broken Shell was buried. They laid her under a cool pandanus tree overlooking the wide, blue sea.

3
Left Shoe Grows Up

LEFT SHOE GREW tall and thin. He was a quiet boy who suffered from bad eyesight. He had to wear glasses when he was only a few months old. Left Shoe knew from the very beginning that he was different from other seadogs. All of his cousins and friends came in pairs. There were Brass Button and Pink Shell, Rusty Wire and Plastic Bottle, Orange Rope and Sinker.

When the other pups played together, they played in pairs. Seadogs do everything that way. The seagrass baskets woven by seadog children require two sets of paws. When they sail their boats on sunny afternoons, it is always a pair of pups in each boat. Left Shoe was alone.

All seadogs go to school, of course. Before they reach their first birthday they begin their lessons. To a human this must sound very young to be starting school, but you must understand that a seadog grows up much faster than you do. For every

human year there are seven seadog years. Left Shoe, for instance, was one-and-a-bit years old at the time of this story, which means he was actually about eight in human years.

On warm days, school is held under the trees, and in cooler weather the children have classes in their own burrow classroom. The teacher shows the young seadogs all kinds of things. As well as reading, writing and sums, they learn basket weaving, sewing, sailing and fishing. These are the skills seadogs need when they are grown-ups. When Left Shoe went to school, he sat by himself. All the other young dogs sat next to their twin, and Left Shoe noticed that they helped each other with their school work. He had to learn to do everything alone. Left Shoe was, just as his name suggests, left out.

Sometimes, when he felt lonely, Left Shoe sailed his little boat out on the open sea. He liked the feel of the breeze ruffling his fur and the swish of

the waves against the bow of the boat. He would gaze dreamily at the horizon. After a while it seemed to matter less that his own twin, Broken Shell, could not be with him.

One such afternoon Left Shoe had been fishing. He glanced at his shining catch sitting in the bucket at the bottom of the boat and wagged his tail. His father would be pleased. Perhaps his mother would cook the fish for supper and serve them with seed cakes and sea cucumber fritters! His tummy growled hungrily

at the thought and he turned his boat towards the shore. He saw with surprise that the sun had nearly disappeared behind the line of trees above his village. It was later than he realised, and he pulled the sails tighter to speed his run home.

His boat scraped the sand and he jumped out. He pulled the little craft up onto the beach, past the tide line, and secured it with the anchor rope. The evening was darkening as he took

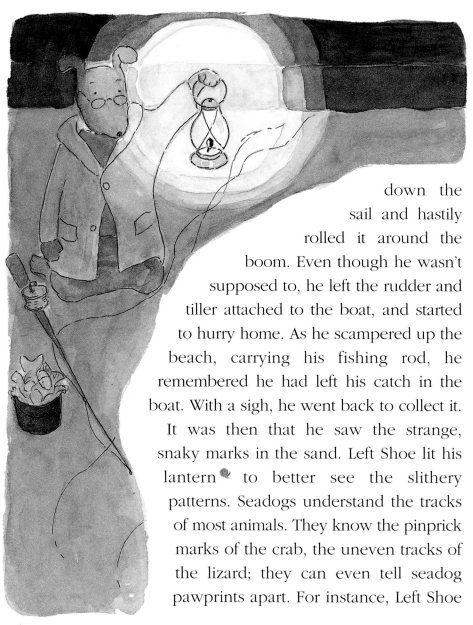

down the sail and hastily rolled it around the boom. Even though he wasn't supposed to, he left the rudder and tiller attached to the boat, and started to hurry home. As he scampered up the beach, carrying his fishing rod, he remembered he had left his catch in the boat. With a sigh, he went back to collect it. It was then that he saw the strange, snaky marks in the sand. Left Shoe lit his lantern to better see the slithery patterns. Seadogs understand the tracks of most animals. They know the pinprick marks of the crab, the uneven tracks of the lizard; they can even tell seadog pawprints apart. For instance, Left Shoe

knew that Old Cork had been looking
for him. Close to the line of boats on the
beach, he saw his father's heavy
footsteps. He looked back to the curling
marks and wondered what creature had
made them. The fur on his back stood
up in fear. Could it be a snake?

He looked around to see if there
was one, slithering behind a clump of
grass. Shadows thickened beyond the
glow of his lantern. Shivering, Left
Shoe picked up the bucket of fish with
one paw and his rod with the other.
He stumbled and ran towards home.
Behind him, the ink-black sea stretched
to the night sky and a gurgling movement disturbed the surface of the
water.

4
The Giant Squid

LEFT SHOE DIDN'T STOP running until he burst through the door, out of breath.

'Great Blue Whale! Where have you been?' Old Cork barked.

'We were worried,' said Blue Bottle. 'It's dark!'

'Sorry, I was fishing,' panted Left Shoe, holding out the bucket of fish for his mother. 'Father,' he continued in a rush, 'I think you should come and see the strange tracks I found on the beach.'

Old Cork stopped work on the fishing net he was mending and turned to him. 'What kind of tracks?'

'Curling,' said Left Shoe, making the movement with his paw, 'like a snake…'

Before he could finish his description, his father had taken the lantern from Left Shoe and gone out into the night.

When Old Cork returned, Left Shoe and Blue Bottle had cleaned and scaled the fresh fish. The first of the fillets sizzled in an iron pan and there were seed cakes warming on top of the stove. Old Cork sat down heavily.

'It's as I suspected. The giant squid has come back. I found five separate places where it has left its mark on the sand.'

Left Shoe turned to his parents. 'What's a giant squid?' he asked.

'Well…' said Old Cork. He looked uncertain, but then widened his mouth into a reassuring smile. 'It's just the same as an ordinary squid, only bigger.'

Being a seadog, Left Shoe had seen many squid pulled up in fishing nets. Barbecued squid was his favourite meal. 'Have you ever seen a giant squid?' he asked.

Blue Bottle had gone very still. Left Shoe saw that her ears were flattened, and that she stared out of the window even though it was dark outside. His father was looking at him strangely.

'Well, Left Shoe… you see… it's your mother. She has seen a giant squid. She saw one as a child.' Old Cork turned to Blue Bottle, who was now busily turning the fish in the pan.

'Was it a giant squid that ate Grandmother?' Left Shoe asked, his eyes round in sudden understanding. He remembered the story his father had told him – that Blue Bottle had seen her own mother taken from the beach by a terrible sea monster. Left Shoe waited for his father to answer, but Old Cork scratched his whiskers and looked towards Blue Bottle. She was lifting plates from the shelf and placing them on the table.

'Is a giant squid a sea monster?' continued Left Shoe, looking from one parent to the other. Old Cork opened his mouth to speak, but Left Shoe interrupted him. 'Didn't you say,' he asked in a rush, 'that a monster with long tentacles –'

There was a loud crash. Left Shoe turned towards the noise and saw his mother standing by the stove. Her eyes had a faraway look in them and the broken pieces of a plate lay at her feet.

'Yes, Left Shoe!' Old Cork said loudly into the sudden silence.

Left Shoe opened his mouth to ask another question, and then thought better of it. Old Cork fetched the broom, and when he had swept up the broken pieces, he came to his wife's side.

'It was long ago,' he said, his voice low and soothing, 'and your mother was very courageous.' He patted his wife's paw and Blue Bottle smiled bravely.

Left Shoe wondered if he should be frightened. He looked at his parents to see if they were worried. His father was bustling about, putting plates of crispy fish and toasted seed cake on the table. As they sat down to eat, Left Shoe saw his mother turn again to the window. She gazed through its dark pane, far out into the night, at the restless movement of the sea.

Later, when Left Shoe had gone to bed, he lay awake

watching the shadows. They seemed to shift in the dark, forming frightening shapes. He rolled over and faced the window, but then became aware of the sighing sound of the trees outside. Their long pale branches waved like tentacles and scratched the shutters spookily. In the distance, the bubbly waves spread across the beach with a soft roar. He couldn't help but think again of those slithery marks, erased by the incoming tide. Where was the giant squid now? Left Shoe imagined its

ghostly body moving silently through the black water. A scurry in the undergrowth outside made him sit up in fright. He could feel his heart thumping. Tossing aside the covers, Left Shoe climbed out of bed and tiptoed towards the light-filled doorway of the cooking-snug. He knew his parents would be cross to see him still awake, so he sat quietly in the semi-darkness, listening to the comforting sound of their voices.

Blue Bottle and Old Cork were drinking squink in the soft chairs by the stove and they spoke in hushed voices.

'I'll go down to the village meeting tree first thing tomorrow and make an announcement. We'll have to get together and come up with a plan,' said Old Cork. He sighed heavily. 'This will mean no fishing, at least not at sea. I hope we have enough in our store-snugs to last until the giant squid has gone.'

Blue Bottle picked up her cup and stared into its inky contents. 'Isn't it strange,' she said. 'The squid is our favourite food. We sip its ink as tea. We eat its tentacles roasted, fried and baked into pies... and yet the giant squid...' Blue Bottle's paws began to tremble and she took a sip of squink. 'It is such a terrifying creature. Some say that it can control the weather and calm wild storms. Whenever the giant squid is about, the water suddenly becomes as flat as a pond, and everything quietens. It's enough to make your fur fall out!' She placed the china cup on its saucer and looked at Old Cork. Her ears were shivering. 'I've even heard that it has special skin that can change colour, and that it... glows.'

'Yes,' said Old Cork, 'I wouldn't like to meet a giant squid at sea. Its arms can capsize boats and the poor sailors are never seen again.'

Left Shoe, overhearing this last horror, began to creep back to the safety of his bed.

He stumbled in the darkness, falling over a basket of washing outside his door.

'Is that you, Left Shoe?' called his mother.

Left Shoe didn't reply, but ran back to bed and dived under the blankets.

The next day, Old Cork called a meeting of all the villagers of Foamy Bay. They gathered on the clearing of grass next to the large fig tree. When Old Cork told them of his discovery, the other seadogs were very frightened. 'Great Blue Whale protect us!' cried someone at the back. The other seadogs barked to each other in alarm.

'All right, everyone,' said Old Cork, raising his paw, 'panicking won't help. We need to decide what we are going to do. I think we should ask the Old Ones.'

The Old Ones sat quietly in their chairs for a moment. They were, of course, the great-great-grandmothers and the great-great-grandfathers of the village. They talked softly to each other and several of them wagged their tails stiffly as they reached an agreement.

One very ancient seadog rose shakily to her feet. Everyone quietened, as she was very old and wise.

'We must stay away from the sea,' she said in her quavery voice. 'We must share our food until the giant squid goes back to the deep water.'

Over the next few months, the seadogs lived in fear of the giant squid. Sailing was forbidden; swimming banned. Now, when the baby seadogs were named, their mothers nursed them from a safe distance. Their worried fathers quickly grabbed their naming treasure, before they all hurried back to the safety of their burrows.

It was a harsh time. The seadogs were too frightened to go fishing in the sea. They had to use the river instead. The river was full of mangroves, whose strange thick roots poked up through the mud and gave off a dank smell. But close to where the little river met the sea, it flowed shallowly over sandbanks, clear, green and salty. There the villagers put out nets, but only managed to catch a few bitter-tasting toadfish. They had to rely on their stores of grass-seed flour, dried fish and pickled sea vegetables. The children caught crabs or gathered fish eggs in the swamp. Whatever food could be found, they shared.

Then, winter began to ease and the warmer weather returned. The seadogs realised that it had been a long time since anyone from Foamy Bay village had seen snaky marks on the sand. Finally, they allowed themselves to hope. One morning the first boat went out to sea, and returned home safely. Soon afterwards, the seadogs of Foamy Bay began to sail out on the deep water once again.

5
Driftwood and Shark Tooth

THAT SPRING, Blue Bottle and Old Cork had another set of twins. It was a bright blue day as they proudly carried their babies to the beach. The little girl was named Shark Tooth when Old Cork found that fierce piece of bone, sharper than glass. Then, Blue Bottle spied a grey plank of driftwood much worn by the sea, smoother than stone. So the little boy was named Driftwood. The other seadogs looked on and smiled now that new happiness had come to the Sandburrow family.

At first Left Shoe was very proud and excited by the arrival of his little brother and sister. He was old enough to help his mother by now, and could dress them and change their nappies.

Sometimes he fed them their seaweed mash and took them for walks outside so his mother could rest.

Baby seadogs grow up quickly. They are a bit like other dogs, as they can walk at only a week old. But seadogs are special, because they can also talk. Most pups say their first word at only two months! Driftwood and Shark Tooth grew fast, and like all twins, they loved to play together.

One afternoon Left Shoe took them for a walk along the beach. He noticed they chased each other in and out of the sand dunes. Driftwood wagged his tail and jumped about with happy barks. Shark Tooth ran around in circles with her ears standing up happily. Somehow they always knew where the other was hiding.

'Chase me!' barked Driftwood.

'I'll catch you!' returned Shark Tooth.

As Left Shoe watched them running on the sand, he felt a bubble of sadness in his chest. I have no one, he thought.

He turned back to the twins. 'Come on then,' called Left Shoe, 'I'm hungry, let's go home.'

'Coming!' they chorused together, scampering up the beach

towards their burrow. As Left Shoe followed, the bubble of sadness grew larger. He looked out to sea and tried to think of something happy, as his mother had told him. But no happy thought came. Instead, he remembered that tomorrow was the school sports day, the day when he always felt more alone than ever.

The next morning, Left Shoe was woken by the smell of freshly baked seed cakes. He rubbed his eyes and put on his glasses. The sad, lonely feeling was still there. He crawled out of bed and dressed reluctantly. He fed his pet seahorse with dried shrimp. The seahorse swam gracefully across the glass bowl and then turned around to look at Left Shoe.

'Hello, Ajax,' said Left Shoe.

Ajax blinked in a dignified fashion and then turned one

goggle eye towards the food. He looked at it for a moment, then swam away. Left Shoe sighed. A seahorse wasn't the same as a proper twin. With a sad growl, he followed the warm smell into the kitchen.

Blue Bottle greeted him with a sleepy bark and handed him some hot seed cakes smothered in butter (sea cow butter, that is) and honey. He looked gloomily at the seed cakes. Not even a delicious breakfast could cheer him up. Old Cork glanced across his cup of squink.

'Morning, Left Shoe,' he barked, before returning his cup to its saucer and straightening out the newspaper.

Driftwood and Shark Tooth were already chattering about the sports day, which was to be held after lunch at the school. Even though they were still too small for school, Driftwood and Shark Tooth were allowed to join in on the sports day. As usual, all of the games and races were in pairs, because, as I told you before, that's just the way it is for seadogs. Left Shoe dreaded it, as he had no partner for anything.

'I'm not going,' Left Shoe announced suddenly.

'You have to!' cried the twins.

'Well,' said Left Shoe, 'I won't be there. I'm going fishing.'

'The sky looks dark, Left Shoe,' said Blue Bottle sensibly. 'I think there could be a storm coming.'

'You can't go out in a storm,' said Driftwood.

Shark Tooth nodded importantly. 'Yes, you might get lost.'

Left Shoe glared at his brother and sister. Everyone seemed to be looking at him. He felt tears prickle behind his eyes. 'I'm going fishing!' yelped Left Shoe. He got up from the table and ran out the door, silently grabbing his fishing rod and waterproof jacket as he went.

Blue Bottle looked to Old Cork for help.

'I suppose it might rain,' he said, looking out of the window. 'But I think he'll be all right. He's a good sailor, you know.' Old Cork returned to his paper for a moment then looked up. Blue Bottle came to his side.

'He'll be all right,' Old Cork said quietly. 'Just let him go.' He squeezed Blue Bottle's paw.

The day was grey but not yet raining as Left Shoe pushed his boat into the water. The sails caught a fresh gust of wind and he hauled in the mainsheet. He reset the jib and the little craft picked up speed. Sea spray wet his fur and a salty breeze flapped his ears. Pulling the tiller towards him, he turned his boat in the direction of the ocean.

'It's just you and me,' Left Shoe whispered to the sea. He fixed his eyes on the long, straight line of the horizon and thought of the fish he would catch. If only he had noticed, back on the beach, the slithery marks on the sand, curling and snaky.

6
Peril at Sea

WHEN LEFT SHOE had sailed beyond sight of the shore and Foamy Bay village, he came to a deep part of the sea where the water was dark blue. Seabirds were wheeling around in the air, which told him that there were fish about. He turned the boat into the wind and took down the sails. Alone on the water, he had already forgotten the sports day. He hummed a little seadog song as he prepared his line for fishing and fetched the jar of bait from the fishing basket. Carefully pulling out a long, grey worm, he attached it, wriggling, to the hook. He was concentrating so deeply that he didn't see the heavy clouds gathering lower in the sky. The first drops of rain

fell in fat splashes and a cold gust of wind blew in from the south. Left Shoe put on his waterproof jacket and threw the line into the dark water.

'It's just a bit of rain,' he said to himself.

The wind grew stronger and the rain started to pelt down. Left Shoe's glasses fogged up so much that he could hardly see. He took them off and folded them neatly into his jacket pocket. He checked his bait and then recast, but the wind blew the line too close to the boat. He tried again, but this time the hook got tangled and the bait was lost. The rain splashed into his eyes and ran down

his nose. It was getting too difficult to fish, so he tidied away his rod in the bottom of the boat. When he had finished he looked about, squinting his eyes through the dark threads of rain. The storm was getting worse. It was all around him; the water found its way under his

jacket, soaking his clothes, and the wind blew so hard it shut his eyes and slapped his ears against his head.

Soon the sea began to heave. A mighty swell tossed the little craft, first into a deep valley of dark water, then to the top of a gigantic, foam-capped wave.

'I'm not afraid of you, storm!' he shouted.

Left Shoe was, as his father said, a good sailor. He had been in storms before and he knew what to do. A sea anchor can give stability to a little boat in heavy seas, so he fetched a bucket from under one of the seats. The boat rocked violently and he fell against the side. He grabbed the mast with both paws as a huge wave splashed across the bow, drenching him. Left  Shoe barked in spite of himself. The water was cold. He held the mast with one arm and searched in the little hold for the rope. When he found it, he closed the round hatch. Every movement took a long time because, with each enormous wave, the little boat was splashed or rocked about sickeningly. Left Shoe attached one end of the rope to the bucket and tied the other end around the base of the mast.

That's how you make a sea anchor. He threw the bucket over the side and it went down, down underneath the water.

In that moment the waves quietened and the swell of the sea grew smaller. Left Shoe, crouched in the bottom of the boat, looked up. At first he thought that the sea anchor had brought about a miracle. He sat up a little more. 'Great Blue Whale!' he exclaimed softly. The waves had now totally disappeared and the sea had become a sheet of green glass. The wind had died, but rain still fell, disturbing the surface of the water. An eerie calm seemed to spread all around. No seagull cried. No fish splashed. The only sound was the soft patter of the rain on the water. Soon that, too, stopped.

The fur on Left Shoe's back prickled in fear. He knew there was only one creature that could quiet a storm – the giant squid! His mind went dark with panic. Around him the quiet deepened.

He crouched back down beside the centreboard and tried to slow his breathing. A sudden soft thump on the side of the boat made him bark in fright. He looked wildly about, his heart pounding. Then, he saw just under the water, right beside the boat, the horror: the giant squid!

Two great glassy eyes glowed greenly; they held Left Shoe in their dreadful stare. Paralysed with shock, Left Shoe tried to look away. Instead, his round-eyed gaze was fixed on the giant squid. The enormous white body of the creature was as big as Left Shoe's boat and the water was full of the writhing mass of its murderous arms. Under each of the snaky arms were lines of round suckers, grey and slimy. Can you imagine anything more terrifying? I think I told you before that each one of those 'o' shaped mouths hides a jagged line of very sharp hooks. They could slice off your finger! Left Shoe saw everything as if it were in slow motion. The gigantic, silent creature floated, spreading its arms wide. He saw the longer feeding tentacles with their hideous clubs covered in greyish suckers. A strange glow emanated from the mollusc's whole body, and as Left Shoe watched in terrified awe, the giant squid began to change colour! Its white body turned to mottled brown, then red, then blue, and the whole monster glowed with a terrible, unearthly

light. Left Shoe could not look away. The giant squid slowly lifted an arm above the surface of the water. Left Shoe sat transfixed as the thick curling arm lifted higher, showing a double line of grey suckers. He knew he was about to be eaten.

There was a sickening thump as the giant squid threw its tentacles across the bow of the boat. The club-tipped ends gave a loud crack and the unexpected noise made Left Shoe jump. He snapped out of his shocked state. He saw the huge, whip-like appendages only a metre from where he crouched. Up close, they were even more horrifying. The tentacles slithered, and their club tips oozed slime from the suckers. What could Left Shoe do? Then, he spied the oar lying next to him. He shifted carefully towards it and slowly pulled it out from under the seat. The club of the tentacle moved further across the bow, scratching the paint with its barbed suckers. Left Shoe lifted the oar and, with all his might, brought it crashing down on the tentacle. It felt good to be fighting back. He bashed it again. Nothing happened. He waited, his breath heaving in and out. Then, summoning all his strength, he raised the oar once more. But before he could strike, the long tentacles slid down under the water.

Left Shoe stood in the middle of the boat, oar raised, his breath now coming in short gasps. He scanned the water frantically, desperately searching for evidence of the giant squid. No ripple troubled the surface of the water; only a deep calm remained. It spread across the glassy sea. Left Shoe turned this way and that, brandishing his oar.

'Come and get me!' he shouted.

It was then that he saw something else floating on the water. It was moving towards him, too big to be a piece of driftwood, too small to be a boat. Before he could make out what it was, the storm came to life again and the waves grew large once more.

7
An Amazing Discovery

LEFT SHOE RETURNED to crouch between the hold in the bow of the boat and the centreboard casing. He wrapped his arms around the mast and braced himself against the churning wash. He thought of his burrow home and wondered if he would live to see it again. He remembered his mother's kind face and round ears; his father's smile. With his paws he held the mast as tightly as he could, and looked across the peaks of the mountainous waves. Judging by the enormous seas, he supposed that the giant squid had gone. He decided that he would have to wait out the storm, as sailing was impossible. He didn't want to end up in the same sea as the giant squid.

It was then that he saw the floating object for a second time. It wasn't a boat; it wasn't a piece of driftwood. It was a basket – the kind of seagrass basket in which baby seadogs sleep. A tall wave rose up out of the sea, lifting it high. When the basket reached the wave's zenith, it skimmed down the other side and Left Shoe lost sight of it behind the rolling swell. Another wave splashed across the bow, soaking him to the skin. Then the basket appeared again on a bubbly bed of foam. It sailed right into the bow. To his surprise, the basket held a tiny, shivering seadog. Left Shoe grabbed the oar to bring the basket alongside. It was a girl puppy, dressed in a yellow spotted nightdress, which was dripping wet.

'Jumping jellyfish,' he barked in astonishment. 'Where did you come from?'

She whimpered a little when Left Shoe picked her up. He
hushed her and placed her underneath his jacket. The little wet
seadog regarded Left Shoe with round eyes. In the warmth of
his coat, he could feel her trembling.

'You'll be all right now,' he said quietly. 'I'll keep you safe.'

Left Shoe had been so busy rescuing the little pup that he
hadn't noticed that there was other flotsam following in the
wake of the basket. Broken pieces of wood clustered together
with a strange variety of things: saucepans and long pieces of
rope, clothes and a hat decorated with flowers. Left Shoe
gazed in wonder at the variety of objects. More chunks of
splintered wood floated into view, as well as a ripped sail and

some long wire stays. Was this a shipwreck? Next to the boat bobbed a vinegar bottle, a toothbrush, a book and a wooden box. The box drifted closer until it bumped the side of the boat. Left Shoe leaned over and fished it out of the water. It was plain, but finely made with a sliding lid. He put it in his fishing basket for safe keeping. Where had all these things come from? He was about to rescue some of the other interesting objects when he realised that something had changed. The sea had become flat again; no breath of wind stirred. For a moment he thought that the storm had passed, but ripples on the sea's glassy surface told another story. The giant squid had returned.

Left Shoe now not only had to save himself, but also the helpless foundling, who was poking her soft nose out of his jacket. Left Shoe looked around, trying to work out where the giant squid was hiding. He could feel its presence, silent and menacing. The little pup wrapped in his jacket began to cry in a high wail. Left Shoe acted quickly. He grabbed the oars and placed them in their rowlocks and then he started to row with all his might. He pulled on the oars, growling with determination. His heart pounded in fear but he tried to calm the little pup.

'Ssshush,' he said bravely. 'I can row very fast. We'll be all right, you'll see.'

He rowed through the flotsam, which bumped against the boat as he passed. He had started to sing out loud to calm himself when he heard a small splash on the starboard side. Left Shoe saw a tentacle break the surface of the water and disappear again. He began to row in the other direction, but in front of him he could see the huge glowing form through the water's murky surface. The creature was only metres from his boat and getting nearer. As he watched, the giant squid began to move in a huge arc, drawing water into its ghastly body then squirting it out in a powerful stream. Propelling the creature forwards, its long tentacles and eight arms followed

the movement. Back and forth they went, in time with each squirting jet of water. It was a fearful ballet, a terrifying dance with its own inner light. The squid's eyes were full of evil intelligence. It circled Left Shoe's boat, coming nearer and nearer.

A dreadful thump echoed in the stillness. The giant squid had cast the feeding tentacles over the side of the boat! They writhed and slithered on the floor of the little craft, twining together to form a living rope. The club-tipped ends joined and then opened as monstrous jaws! Left Shoe stumbled back in utter panic. He tried to get as far as he could from those murderous sharp teeth. He perched on the opposite side of the boat, holding on desperately to the stays. The foundling shot out of Left Shoe's jacket and scrambled on to his shoulders, barking in terror. The mollusc now unfurled two of its suckered arms. They curled upwards, finding the mast and encircling it like a python gripping its prey. Slowly, the boat was pulled towards starboard. It tipped up on its side, higher and higher. Left Shoe was lifted into the air. He leaned right out in a desperate attempt to balance the boat, but it was no use. The giant squid was a thousand times stronger. Left Shoe's boat capsized. The little baby seadog jumped from Left Shoe's shoulders and scurried along the high side of the boat, yapping and barking in terror. Left Shoe wasn't so fortunate. He fell backwards into the sea with a splash.

8
The Great Blue Whale

THE COLD WATER
made Left Shoe gasp.
Directly underneath
him he could see the squid's
writhing arms moving in the
greenish water. He came to the
surface behind the underside
of the boat. Above him, he
heard the little seadog barking
loudly. Left Shoe swam towards the
centreboard, which was sticking out
sideways. The giant squid felt the
movement in the water and unfurled its
tentacles, ready to strike. Left Shoe
grasped the centreboard and climbed the
underside of the boat. He slipped in
panic, then scampered up again. Finally,

HOOOOOOWLLLLLOOWOWOOWW

HOOOHOO HOOOWOO
HOWOOOOOWLLLHOWHOWHOOOOOWWWWWLLL

he reached the top of the boat's upturned side, where the little baby seadog was waiting for him. She barked at him with her high-pitched yap and Left Shoe barked back. Together they crouched, clinging to the boat with their claws. Below them, the giant squid was swimming in a large arc, drawing a luminous circle around Left Shoe's boat. Its green eyes were full of malice. It swam slowly, as if it were

LL HOWHOW HOOOO L LLOW HOWWOWOO/Woo oow LL Ow ooow HOOOW LL

taking a moment to savour the final strike.

Left Shoe took a deep breath. He was determined to save the little seadog. He lifted his nose to the sky and let out a fierce howl. It wasn't an ordinary howl. It was a bold howl, a brave howl, a howl that filled the sea and sky. Left Shoe called to the ancient seadog protector, the largest creature on the earth, the Great Blue Whale. While Left Shoe howled, the giant squid came ever

LLHOW HOW WWOW OOWOOOW L L HOOOW

nearer, an eerie glow emanating from its pale body. The little pup joined in, adding her piping voice to Left Shoe's. Their plaintive calls travelled far across the sea to the Indian Ocean.

'Hoooowww-hooowwwwwl! Hoooowwwl-hoooooaaauuul! Hooooowwwww Hooouuuuaaaaalll Hooowwooowwlll!'

Left Shoe and the foundling howled without stopping; they howled in a wailing cacophony of notes. They howled and they howled until suddenly, there was a mighty splash. The great tail of a blue whale punctured the calm water in a tall arc of sea spray.

Left Shoe gasped in wonder. He had never seen a creature as beautiful and majestic. The whale was so large that it was like an island when it broke the surface of the water. The beautiful creature called to Left Shoe in a low rumble. It was a deep note, lower than any you could imagine.

'Great Blue Whale!' Left Shoe whispered.

A flipper, three metres long, was lifted towards him.

Left Shoe and the foundling, perched on the side of the upturned boat, gazed in silent awe. Only metres away, two of the most enormous creatures on earth prepared for a great sea battle.

The giant squid, who had been slowly swimming around the boat, turned towards the whale and drew up its tentacles. Before it could strike, the blue whale thrashed its muscular tail at the creature's head and missed. The giant squid attacked,

shooting its club-tipped tentacles at the whale. The jagged barbs protruded from the rows of suckers and hooked into the whale's side, drawing blood. The mighty whale fought back, turning around and around in the water, churning the sea into a whirlpool. It drew back its powerful tail and then straightened it with such force that the squid was catapulted through the water. Then the whale pounded the monster with its tail. Each blow caused a huge white-capped wave, which nearly swamped the little boat.

Left Shoe held on with all four paws, his claws clinging to the upturned side. The little seadog sat close to him. At that moment Left Shoe felt even more frightened. He was worried that the sheer power of the contest between the Great Blue Whale and the giant squid would kill them. Then, as if the whale could read his thoughts, the enormous animal turned and dived downwards to the very depths of the ocean. The giant squid followed it to the darkest bottom of the sea.

Left Shoe watched as the blue whale and the giant squid disappeared under the water. Here was his chance. He placed the pup on his shoulders.

'Hold on,' he told her. 'Put your paws around my neck and don't let go!'

When the pup was holding on tightly, he climbed down the underside of the boat and stood on the centreboard. Using all his strength he rocked back and forth. With each push the boat came closer to an upright position. Finally it came to rest on the surface the right way up. There was only one problem; the bottom of the boat was full of water.

Left Shoe looked for the giant squid and the Great Blue Whale. He could see no sign of them, but he knew they must be deep under the sea, fighting to the death. Perhaps he would have a few moments to bail out the boat. He remembered that the bucket was still being used as a sea anchor. He frantically pulled it up, hauling on the long rope. When it reached the surface he began bailing as quickly as he could. Soon the water level dropped. The little pup clung to his shoulders, barking to urge him on. Left Shoe gently pulled her paws from his neck.

'You're not going to like this,' he said, 'but it's for your own safety.' He opened the hatch in the bow and placed the pup in the little hold. He shut the hatch, leaving a crack for the foundling to look through.

'You stay there,' he said. 'I'll come and get you when it's safe.'

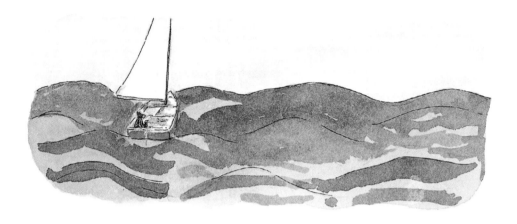

Left Shoe raised the mainsail and pulled in the sheet.

'Please let there be some wind,' he said to himself. He looked at the sky for any sign of the storm, but the dark clouds seemed to have lifted. He let the sail out wide. A puff of wind tickled his whiskers. He pushed the tiller again, looking for the direction of the breeze. Another gust filled the sail, which flapped and caught some wind on its other side. The breeze pushed him forwards, away from the place of the great sea battle. A huge splash broke the surface of the water behind him.

The two gigantic creatures were locked in combat, and the tranquil water now churned with splashing waves. A bleeding line of scratches along the whale's side showed the mark of the giant squid. The monster was again wrapped around the blue whale, who responded by rolling over and over, whirling in the water. The giant squid's clubbed tentacles loosened. The whale worked the water into a storm of white foamy waves. It

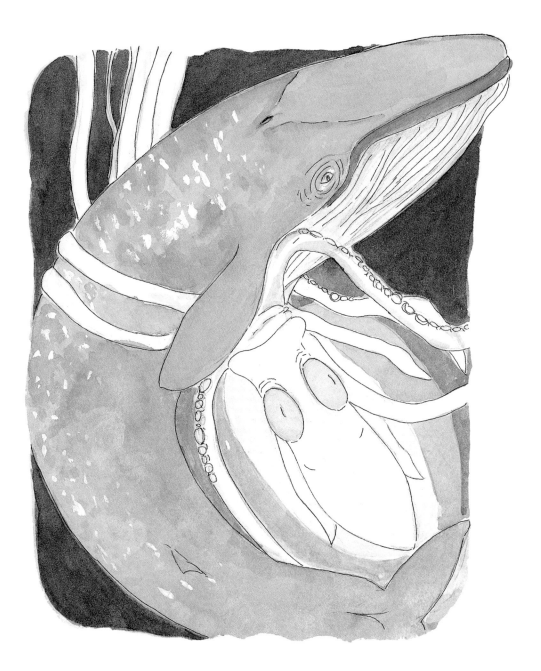

thrashed its marvellous tail again, and the giant squid was shaken off at last. In desperation, the monster sucked sea water into its body with a ghastly gurgling sound. Then it squirted a huge black jet of ink at the whale. Left Shoe watched in amazement as the water filled instantly with murky clouds. The squid tried to hide behind its screen, but the whale was too quick. In a final display of mightiness, the tail of that awesome blue whale rose up out of the water, higher than the mast of Left Shoe's boat, and then came crashing down on the cursed creature.

The wash from the final strike was so big that, in fear of capsizing again, Left Shoe turned the boat to meet it head on. The craft crashed through its foamy crest, the splash of the spray soaking Left Shoe anew. After a few moments the waves died down and there was quiet. Not an eerie quiet as before, but an everyday kind of quiet. He turned his boat into the wind and let the sail flap. Was it really over? There was no sign of the giant squid. Left Shoe wasn't sure if he wanted to laugh or cry. Then, the whale rose to the surface with a triumphant whoosh from its blowhole.

'Thank you,' Left Shoe said in a hushed voice. The Great Blue Whale turned sideways, breaking the surface of the water. Left Shoe could see one kind eye looking at him wisely. Left Shoe looked back. The blue whale's gentle expression filled him with peace. Holding Left Shoe's gaze, the Great Blue Whale moved down beneath the water, singing in its low, rumbling voice. Left Shoe watched until the beautiful giant was out of sight.

Some distance away, the enormous body of the giant squid drifted lifelessly on the surface. Its malevolent eyes had gone dark and a huge slick of black squid ink floated all around it.

A knocking sound brought Left Shoe back to the present. It was coming from the hold in the bow of the boat. The baby seadog wanted to come out. Left Shoe barked in reply.

'I'm coming,' he called. When he opened the hatch, the pup leapt out and crawled under Left Shoe's jacket, trembling.

'It's all right now,' he said to the little foundling. 'The giant squid is dead.'

Left Shoe could see that the squid wasn't moving. Then he had an idea. If he were to bring it home, the seadogs would have enough food for an enormous feast! Left Shoe sailed towards the spreading ink.

The tentacles splayed out around the creature, framing the head like hideous hair. He could see a long gash between its sightless eyes, which showed the dark insides. The little dog in his arms barked loudly at it, and Left Shoe laughed. He and the pup looked at each other. She lifted her ears and then folded one over (which is hello in the language of Earlish), and Left Shoe smiled. It was nice to have someone to talk to. Then all at once he knew what it must be like to have your own twin, your one true friend. It felt just right for a seadog. He placed the foundling carefully in the bottom of the boat.

'You wait there,' Left Shoe said. He leaned out to check that the squid was really dead. Even though he could see that it was, he poked it with the oar just in case. The squid didn't move.

'Completely dead,' he said, turning to the pup. 'Utterly, totally dead.'

The little baby yapped in reply.

Left Shoe found the strong length of rope he had used for the sea anchor. With this he bound several of the squid's tentacles together. He was very careful to avoid the suckers and their hidden hooks. He secured the binding with a double

knot, and tied the other end of the rope to the boat. He retrieved the jib from the hold and hoisted it into position. He would need every bit of wind to tow the squid. Next he found his compass in his jacket pocket. Its wobbly needle swung northwards and Left Shoe carefully worked out the way back to Foamy Bay. Then, he lifted the pup and placed her on the seat next to him and let the mainsail out to run before the wind. Left Shoe regarded the little seadog by his side. Her nightdress, he noticed, was drying in the sun, and she gazed happily about her. She looked up at him and caught his eye. Left Shoe smiled. The wind was bringing them home with their magnificent catch.

There would be a feast tonight – barbecued squid, roasted squid, boiled squid! They would celebrate with dancing and seaweed wine, and all of the children would be allowed to stay up late. There would be fresh squink for breakfast and the whole village would help to make the rest of the creature into many things. They would prepare squid pickle (a savoury jam loved by seadog babies), they would soak the squid in lemon juice, then salt it in jars, or dry it on lines in the sun. They would make medicines from the squid ink and the huge eyes. They would even extract a vital ingredient used for whitewash to paint the walls of their snugs!

Left Shoe was now in sight of the shore and could see Foamy Bay village. He pulled his glasses out of his pocket to get a better look at the beach. Even from that distance, he could make out the broken branches and torn vegetation caused by the storm. A little cluster of seadogs was gathering on the sand. The pup had burrowed back into the safety of Left Shoe's jacket with only her nose showing. As the boat neared the beach, Left Shoe could see the separate faces of his whole family coming towards the water's edge. Aunts and uncles, cousins and grandparents crowded round. In moments, other seadogs joined them, waving their paws and barking.

His parents were in the front of the throng. They came running towards him, holding Driftwood and Shark Tooth tightly. Left Shoe reached the shallows, where he was close enough to see his father's worried frown and the pale face of his mother.

9
The Happy Ending

'IT'S THE GIANT SQUID!' shrieked one of the villagers. Some of the seadogs ran up the beach, howling. Blue Bottle froze. She stared at the hideous creature, its floating arms and its terrible eyes. Old Cork, uncertain that the monster was dead, turned to Blue Bottle.

'I'll go,' he said, handing Shark Tooth to her.

Blue Bottle nodded, settling her daughter on the other hip. The rest of the seadogs watched fearfully as Old Cork approached the little craft, now coming in to land.

Left Shoe, grinning broadly, jumped out of the boat.

'The giant squid is dead!' he shouted. Old Cork was already splashing into the water to meet him.

'We thought you had perished in the storm,' said Old Cork. His face wrinkled in concern and he put his arm around Left Shoe's shoulder. 'We were about to send out a search party.' He led Left Shoe up the beach to where his mother stood.

'The giant squid is dead,' said Left Shoe to his mother.

Blue Bottle was overcome with tears. She placed the twins in Old Cork's arms and pulled Left Shoe into a fierce hug.

A muffled bark came from inside his jacket. Blue Bottle released him with a puzzled expression. The high-pitched yap sounded again. Her eyes widened as she spotted a moving lump under Left Shoe's clothes. Left Shoe began to giggle.

'Hey, that tickles,' he said, reaching into his jacket. He lifted out the baby seadog and handed her to his mother. Blue Bottle was amazed.

'Where did you come from?' she asked. The little pup lifted her ears and then folded one down.

'Look, Old Cork, she already speaks Earlish,' said Blue Bottle with a watery smile. She tucked the little seadog into the crook of her arm and then her face grew grave. She furrowed her brow and put her ears back. Turning to Left Shoe she said, 'We had such a terrible storm here, we were so worried about you!' She clasped him in another hug just for good measure, while Old Cork patted his shoulder proudly. The little seadog was

squeezed between them and she barked in
protest. Left Shoe's parents stood back,
smiling broadly now.

'You killed the giant squid!' said his
father, shaking his ears in amazement.

'No, the Great Blue Whale did,' said
Left Shoe solemnly. 'The Great Blue
Whale helped me when I called.'

Old Cork and Blue Bottle wanted to know the whole story
all at once.

'What about the little pup?' asked Blue Bottle, cradling the
baby in her arms.

'Where did you find her?' added Old Cork.

'I found her floating in a basket at sea,' replied Left Shoe.
'She was all alone. I think there might have been a shipwreck,
as there was flotsam everywhere.'

Old Cork was about to ask another question when a little
high-pitched yap distracted him. The foundling sat up and
looked at Blue Bottle with her wide, brown eyes. She really
was the sweetest baby, and believe me, I would know! She
smiled again, lifting her ears. Blue Bottle lifted hers in return,
and Old Cork wagged his tail.

One of the other seadogs called out to Left Shoe. They had
surrounded his little boat and were discussing the giant squid,
barking to each other excitedly. Left Shoe joined the group and

helped them to untie the squid, which was still attached to the back of his boat. They left it floating in the shallows, ready to be cleaned. Because of its enormous size they would have to cut it into smaller portions before it could be taken from the water. The ink sacs would have to be carefully removed, as well as the precious eyes. The beach was a flurry of activity. There were seadogs running about everywhere. Some were already preparing tubs and pots of squeezed bush lemons in which to marinate the squid's arms and tentacles. Some gathered wood for the enormous barbecue, others lined up baskets in which to collect the squid that would be dried or pickled. They would all work hard for the rest of the day, thinking of the party that would come afterwards, and of fresh squink for tomorrow's breakfast.

Left Shoe pulled his boat onto the sand and began to de-rig it. Many seadogs came past and slapped Left Shoe on the

back, shook his paw or ruffled his ears. 'Amazing!' they said. 'Incredible!' His friends from school gathered around asking questions or watching him admiringly.

'You defeated the giant squid!' his cousin Brass Button exclaimed.

'You saved Foamy Bay!' said Float, a pretty girl from his class. Left Shoe's ears went pink from all the attention. When he had finished de-rigging the boat, he went to find his family.

Blue Bottle and Old Cork were sitting a little apart from the crowd and he ran over to meet them. The baby was lying in his mother's lap, fast asleep.

'The poor thing was starving,' Blue Bottle whispered. 'I gave her a jar of squid pickle and then she went straight to sleep.'

Left Shoe sat down next to Old Cork, who was looking out to sea. Old Cork ruffled Left Shoe's ears.

'I just can't believe you're safely home!' He put his arm around him and they all sat quietly for a moment. Driftwood and Shark Tooth came running up the beach, barking.

'Ssshh,' said Left Shoe, 'you'll wake her.'

Old Cork looked questioningly at Blue Bottle. Blue Bottle smiled in agreement. Then Old Cork said to his other children, 'This child is a foundling. She has come to us from the sea.

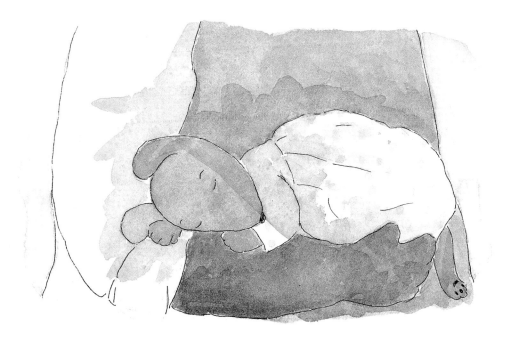

I think we should take her into our burrow and look after her. What do you think?'

Left Shoe could not speak for happiness. He grinned widely and barked. The little baby looked up for a second, opening one eye. Then she snuggled back down in Blue Bottle's lap and went back to sleep.

As soon as they had decided to take in the foundling, Blue Bottle and Old Cork wanted to tell the rest of the village. They carried the sleeping baby over to where the other seadogs were busy with the squid. Old Cork raised his voice.

'Friends,' he announced, 'this child is lost. We would like to look after her until her own parents are found. We will take her into the Sandburrow family.'

'You must name her then,' offered one of the seadogs. The little pup, only a few weeks old, was too young to know her own name, so received another one that day.

'I know, Father,' said Left Shoe, suddenly remembering the mysterious flotsam. He fetched the wooden box from his fishing basket.

'This box was floating nearby when I found her.'

Old Cork took the box from Left Shoe and carefully opened the lid. Inside it was divided into sections. One of the compartments held a piece of animal skin with soft fur and a sewing needle made out of bone. A miniature portrait of a seadog wearing a strange fur hat filled another. There were some waterlogged letters, which were stuck together in a wet lump. They were impossible to read because the ink had run. Another section held a very pretty brooch in the shape of a flower, a bright orange marigold. Left Shoe picked it up and it flashed in the sunlight. Old Cork nodded.

'I name you Marigold,' said Old Cork in a glad voice.

'Welcome, Marigold, to the Sandburrow family!' said Blue Bottle, smiling. Marigold woke up then and looked up at Left Shoe. Left Shoe stroked her soft ears.

You can probably guess what happened next. Of course there was a huge bonfire, and enough barbecued squid to feed all twenty-three hungry families. As they ate together, the seadogs listened over and over to Left Shoe's amazing story. The young dogs wanted to hear all about the great sea battle. The grown-ups never got tired of listening again to the miraculous rescue of little Marigold. And the old ones begged him to repeat, in every detail, his astonishing encounter with the Great Blue Whale.

Later, when the dancing and eating were over, the Sandburrow family sat in the warmth of the fire's glow. Driftwood and Shark Tooth had already fallen asleep, wrapped in a quilt. Left Shoe gazed into the flames. In his mind the events of that incredible day replayed in vivid pictures. He was so tired that every bone in his body ached. But the lonely feeling had gone. He felt a soft wave of contentment gather around him. Marigold snuggled close, her head against his side, sleeping soundly.

Epilogue

So, that ends the story of Left Shoe and the foundling. Tales of his bravery at sea and the defeat of the giant squid have been recounted in seadog burrows ever since. The foundling grew quickly, as seadogs do, and soon could join Left Shoe in games, and at school. Marigold is happy in the Sandburrow family. How do I know this? Because it's me, of course! Marigold Sandburrow.

THE END

Marigold's Dictionary

Interesting facts by Marigold

Boat *noun*

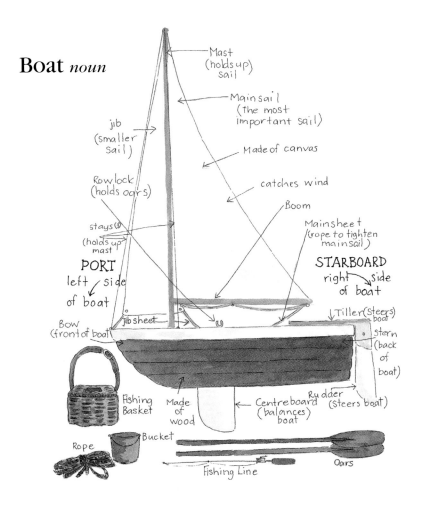

Mast (holds up) sail

Mainsail (the most important sail)

jib (smaller sail)

Made of canvas

Rowlock (holds oars)

catches wind

Boom

stays (3) (holds up mast)

Mainsheet (rope to tighten mainsail)

PORT left side of boat

STARBOARD right side of boat

Tiller (steers) boat

Bow (front of boat)

jib sheet

stern (back of boat)

Fishing Basket

Made of wood

Centreboard (balances) boat

Rudder (Steers boat)

Rope

Bucket

Fishing Line

Oars

Claws *noun* All seadogs have claws hidden in their paws. Claws are useful for holding on to things, digging, climbing trees and basket weaving.

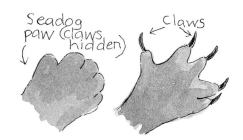

Seadog
paw (claws hidden)

Claws

Flotsam *noun* Flotsam is the floating wreckage of a ship.

water
jar
book
box
clothing
bottle
splintered wood
spoon

Giant squid *noun* The giant squid grows up to twenty metres long and can weigh three thousand kilograms. It has the biggest eyes of the animal kingdom and is thought to have special skin that can glow and change colour.

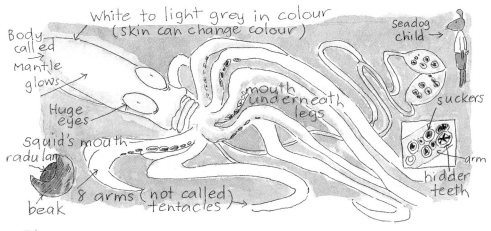

white to light grey in colour (skin can change colour)

Body called Mantle glows

Huge eyes

squid's mouth radula

beak

8 arms (not called) tentacles

mouth underneath legs

seadog child

suckers

arm

hidden teeth

74

Great Blue Whale *noun* The
Great Blue Whale is a special whale
that has protected seadogs since
ancient times. Seadogs believe that the
Great Blue Whale has magical powers,
and howl to it in times of danger.
Seadogs consider sightings of the
creature to be very special.

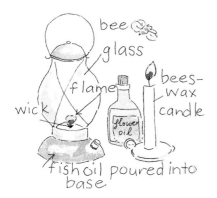

Lantern *noun* Seadogs use fish oil
to burn in their lanterns, sweetened
with flower oil to hide the smell.
They use beeswax for the candles.
(Seadogs are good beekeepers.)

Round hole *noun* Also called a
'wag'. These are found in the back of
seadog trousers and underwear for
tail comfort. Boy seadogs show their
tail to communicate in Waglish,
which is the language of wags. Girl
seadogs communicate in Earlish, the
language of ears.

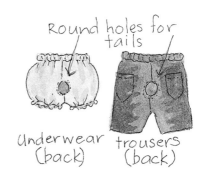

75

Seadog treasure *noun* Any object found washed up on the beach, shore, tide line, or at sea is treasure to seadogs.

Seadog years *noun* Seadogs grow up quickly – there are seven seadog years for every one human year. They become teenagers at two years old! Seadogs live until they are about twenty.

Seed cakes *noun* Seadogs eat seed cakes with every meal. They are made with the flour of grass seeds.

Squink *noun* Squink is a drink made from squid ink. The ink is dried into flakes or taken fresh. When hot water is added it makes a lovely cup of tea.

seaweed sugar

Squink pot

SUGAR

Squid ink

Sea cow milk

fresh squink

dried squink

Snug *noun* A snug is a room in a seadog burrow. There are many snugs in a seadog burrow.

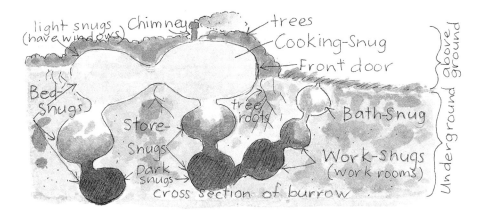

light snugs (have windows)

Chimney

trees

Cooking-Snug

Front door

Bed Snugs

tree roots

Bath-Snug

Store- Snugs

Dark snugs

Work-Snugs (work rooms)

above ground

Underground

cross section of burrow

Whales *noun*

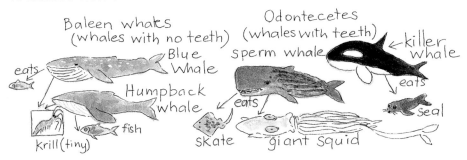

Baleen whales (whales with no teeth)

Odontecetes (whales with teeth)

Blue Whale

sperm whale

killer whale

eats

eats

Humpback whale

eats

seal

fish

krill (tiny)

skate

giant squid

For my own pups - Thomas, Imogen and Kitty

*Thank you to my parents, my family, my friends
and everyone who helped and encouraged me, especially Stephen,
Helen M, Charlie W, Peter M, Aunty Jane, David,
Jonathan, Mrs Thomas and Anna M.*

Visit: www.seadogs.com.au
First published in the UK in 2007
by the National Maritime Museum, Greenwich, London, SE10 9NF

www.nmm.ac.uk/publishing

First published 2005 in Macmillan by
Pan Macmillan Australia Pty Limited,
St Martins Tower, 31 Market Street, Sydney

ISBN 978 0 948065 86 6

1

A CIP record for this book is available from the British Library.

Typeset in 13/18 pt Garamond by Seymour Designs
Jacket design by Seymour Designs
Printed in China